SMART GIRLS FOREVER

Whether you're a smart girl or a smart boy, these sharp-witted stories from around the world will keep you on your toes!

Robert Leeson is one of the most highly regarded writers of fiction for young people. His many books include *Smart Girls* (shortlisted for the 1994 Guardian Children's Fiction Award), *Lucky Lad* and *Why's the Cow on the Roof?*. He also wrote five stories about Grange Hill, based on characters from the popular television series. He has run many workshops for children in schools and in 1985 received the Eleanor Farjeon Award for his services to children's literature.

Books by the same author

Lucky Lad
Smart Girls
Why's the Cow on the Roof?

Smart Girls Forever

ROBERT LEESON

Illustrations by

AXEL SCHEFFLER

WALKER BOOKS
AND SUBSIDIARIES
LONDON • BOSTON • SYDNEY

For Joanna, Mia and Suzannah

ACKNOWLEDGEMENTS

Another, longer version
of the "Marian" tale has appeared
in Robert Leeson's *The Story of Robin Hood*
(Kingfisher, 1994)

"The Little Slippers of Louse Leather" appears in
Russian Folktales (G. Bell, 1971)

First published 1996 by Walker Books Ltd
87 Vauxhall Walk, London SE11 5HJ

This edition published 1997

2 4 6 8 10 9 7 5 3

Text © 1996 Robert Leeson
Illustrations © 1996 Axel Scheffler

The right of Robert Leeson to be identified as author
of this work has been asserted by him in accordance with the
Copyright, Designs and Patents Act 1988.

This book has been typeset in Plantin.

Printed in England

British Library Cataloguing in Publication Data
A catalogue record for this book
is available from the British Library.

ISBN 0-7445-5249-4

Contents

Smart girls – there's no end to them. They're bold, they're outrageous. They defy danger, death, robbers, giants, slavery and sorcery (though they'll make magic themselves at the drop of a hat).

They range the world, on foot, on horseback, even on goat-back, through greenwood, desert or mountains. And if the landscape doesn't meet their needs, they alter it.

Smart Girls rescue brothers, lovers, husbands. They fight their way into – and out of – outlaw bands. They become rulers of distant cities and even outwit the Devil himself.

They are Russian, Indian, Irish, Scottish, Persian and English. They could be from anywhere.

They've always been around and they always will be.

Smart girls forever!

Natasha

Natasha

Natasha was a princess. But she was more than that. She was a winsome wench with a head full of comical fancies.

One day she was combing her long black hair when out popped a louse. She picked it up between her thumb and forefinger and was just about to go "crick" and do away with it, when suddenly she took a fancy to keep it instead.

"No," said she. "You must be a royal louse. So I shall keep you."

And the louse answered, "Thank you kindly, Ma'am."

Natasha was not in the least surprised because her head was full of comical fancies. So she kept the louse and it grew and grew, until it was as big as a mouse.

A louse as big as a mouse cannot be hid,

but Natasha was not at a loss. She carried it out to the royal pasture and put it on a sheep. Every day she went to the flock and talked to the royal louse of this and that, for the louse was both witty and wise.

And if servants saw her there, talking to no one, they just smiled. For it was well known that she was full of comical fancies.

Time passed. Natasha grew more winsome and the louse grew as well, until it was as big as a pup. Natasha was not bothered in the slightest. She shifted it on to a ram, the biggest in the flock.

Soon enough, Natasha grew from a winsome wench into a lovely lady. Yet her head was still full of comical fancies.

As for the louse, it was now as large as a rabbit and Natasha shifted it on to the back of the billy goat. He was lord of the royal herd and as big as a pony with hair like a rug.

All went well and no one guessed Natasha's secret. But one morning she went out into the paddock and there, to her great sadness, she found the louse lying on its back, legs in the air, dead as a doornail.

Still Natasha did not mourn. Instead she had the louse skinned and a pair of slippers made of the hide – as supple and shining as the finest leather.

Which was all very fine. Finer still, she found that the slippers of louse leather could talk as well and they were just as witty and wise as the louse had ever been.

Now, about this time, her father told Natasha, "Time for you to get married my dear."

"But I'm happy as I am, Father," said she.

The Czar frowned, then growled, "Don't be absurd, all princesses get married."

"But I'm different, Father."

The Czar glowered, then roared, "Do as I say, Natasha!"

Now Natasha was a dutiful daughter. She lowered her eyes and looked down at her feet. The slippers of louse leather twinkled at her and a comical fancy came into her head.

"Very well, Father. I will marry the man who can guess what my slippers are made of."

And so a proclamation was made to the four corners of the land. All the hopeful young men flocked to the palace where Natasha smiled sweetly and asked each suitor, "What are the royal slippers made of?"

"Doeskin," said the first suitor.

"Oh, no," answered Natasha.

"Calfskin," said the second.

"Oh, no," answered Natasha.

"Sealskin," said the third suitor.

And so it went on. Every creature under the sun was suggested by the suitors, but the princess just shook her handsome head and the young men departed, broken-hearted.

Until one tall fellow in a flowing red cloak stepped forward and called out, "The slippers are made of louse leather."

"Oh, no," chorused the courtiers, aghast.

"Oh, yes," admitted Natasha woefully.

"That's your husband," said the Czar.

"Very well," said Natasha, looking at her

feet where the slippers were twinkling at her. "But I must have two months' grace to prepare myself."

She had good reason. For while looking at her own feet she had studied those of her suitor. And inside his elegant shoes she had spotted two feet that reminded her of the old billy goat's. She guessed that her intended husband was none other than the Devil himself.

Not for one moment had Natasha thought of getting married. And not for a second did she intend to be Old Nick's loving wife. So while the palace prepared for the wedding, she talked privately to her slippers and soon she knew what to do.

The wedding day dawned fine and sunny. Inside the great hall, tables were decked and at the top table sat the princess, pale and beautiful in her wedding dress, face hidden in her veil.

Along the road came a rollicking crowd, the wedding guests led by the fiendish bridegroom, his red cloak flying in the wind, his wicked face grinning. At the palace door they stopped, however, for the way was blocked by a great billy goat, horns sharp and curved, hair long as a rug.

"Where is the bride, Mr Goat?" they asked.

"In the kitchen, baking," the goat seemed to answer. "Pray wait a while." And with that he trotted off across the palace lawn.

The guests made themselves at home, drinking vodka and singing, till the bridegroom grew restless.

"Where's the bride, Mr Goat?" he called, and the goat shouted back, "Busy in the bedroom, dressing. Wait a while, your honour." And with that he trotted away across the pasture.

The guests carried on drinking and sing-ing until the husband-to-be lost patience. Marching into the hall, he saw Natasha sitting at the table.

"Why did you keep me waiting, hussy?" he raged. But answer came there none. So the

Devil seized the bride by the shoulders. The wedding dress fell down and there in the chair was a large brush over which clothes and veil had been draped.

Old Nick was aflame with fury. He'd been tricked, but quick as lightning he guessed what had happened. Natasha had been hiding on the goat's back among all that hair.
He ran from the hall, across the lawn, over the park and into the pasture. Far off over the rolling meadow he saw the billy goat galloping.

Anger gave him speed. He flew over the ground and soon gained on his fleeing bride.

"Who's coming there?" asked Natasha from the back of her hairy steed, and the louse-leather slippers answered, "Your disappointed bridegroom. Throw down your comb!"

Natasha cast away her comb. At once it grew into a thick thorn forest, which trapped her pursuer while the goat bounded on, mile after mile.

Soon, though, Old Nick struggled free and the chase began again.

"Who's coming there?" called Natasha.

"Your angry would-be husband," answered the slippers. "Throw down a stone!"

Natasha hurled a stone behind her which sprang up like a mountain range, while the goat bounded on, mile after mile.

In his rage their pursuer smashed the mountains to powder and soon Natasha heard his footsteps once more.

"Who's coming there?" she cried and the louse slippers answered, "The Devil himself. Empty your water bottle!"

Straight away a torrent roared between her and the panting bridegroom. But now he had to stop and change his tune.

"Natasha, sweet one," he wheedled. "I can't swim. Help me over and I'll never trouble you any more."

"Throw out your handkerchief," said the slippers. The handkerchief streamed out across the river and the Devil caught hold.

"Pull me over, my lovely," he pleaded.

Natasha hauled away, drawing the Devil over the torrent and, as he came closer, she saw a change in his face. He laughed triumphantly. "Aha, Natasha, you'll be mine forever!"

"Let go," whispered the slippers and so Natasha did. Down went her suitor into the water, foaming and hissing.

So Natasha was a widow before she was wed, and rode home to the palace on the billy goat's back, her head full of comical fancies.

As far as I know, it is to this day.

Yamuna

Yamuna

....

One evening three maidens sat together
eating cakes and sharing secrets. The oldest
one said, "Let us tell our dreams."

The second answered, "You begin."

"Very well. I dream that I have married the
king's treasurer and wear gowns of gold."

Then the second girl spoke. "I dream that I
have married the commander-in-chief and
look down from my balcony at the ranks of
soldiers drawn up below."

They laughed and nudged each other, then
turned to the youngest, who did not speak
but only blushed and shook her head.

"Come now," said the oldest, a little sharply.
"We have told our dreams. Tell us yours."

After a long, long silence, the girl raised her
head. "I dream I shall marry the king and
have two children, a boy, Chandra, with the

moon on his forehead, and a girl with the sun in her eyes. Her name shall be Yamuna."

So surely did she speak that the others were shocked and looked around in fear. "The king! You are shameless. Thank heavens no one has heard."

But someone had. A tall and stately man, disguised as a merchant, had been wandering the city. He had paused by their window and heard all that was said. Having heard, he stole away into the darkness.

Next day the three were summoned to the palace. They went in awe and fear and bowed down before the throne, trembling. But the king said in a kindly voice, "Rise. Be of good cheer. Today your dreams come true. You," he beckoned the oldest, "shall marry my treasurer," and to the second, "you shall marry my commander-in-chief."

Astonished but proud, the two stepped forward as the court applauded. The youngest was left alone at the rear of the great hall. She waited and waited.

At last the king said, "Come forward, my dear. You shall be my wife and we shall have a son and a daughter."

To great cheers she took her place at the king's side. Her eyes were cast down and she did not see the hatred in the eyes of her one-time friends.

Those who are good and happy are blind to envy. So when a year had passed and the young queen was to give birth to her first child, she begged the treasurer's wife and the commander's wife to be with her when the time came.

At dead of night a boy was born. The bedchamber filled with a strange silver light, from the crescent mark on his forehead.

"It has come true," said the commander's wife, amazed. But the treasurer's wife answered, "Quiet, you fool. No one must know of this. She's proud enough as the king's wife. Once she sees this marvellous boy she'll be prouder still."

"What can we do?"

"I'll tell you. Go quickly and secretly to the kitchen. The cook's dog has had pups. Bring one and place it by her side. Then go to the king and tell him, weeping and wailing, that the queen has given birth to a dog."

"I'll do it. But, the baby?"

"Leave that to me."

When the king heard the terrible news, he was beside himself with shame and rage. He ordered that it be proclaimed the child had died. Despite her heartbroken pleas, he would neither talk to nor look at his queen.

And the baby? He was wrapped in a cloth and thrown into the river to drown.

Still, his time had not come. The water carried him along to a garden outside the city walls. In the dawn the gardener spotted the floating bundle and lifted it from the water. He and his wife gazed at the boy in wonder.

"He is like a little god," said she. ·

"He is sent from Heaven," answered he.

"We shall keep him. Let us call him Chandra, because of the moon on his forehead. We can pretend he is our child, but we must hide that mark."

A year went by. The king so wished for an heir, he allowed his wife to come back to the palace and soon the news came that she was to have another child.

Yet she, in her innocence, suspected nothing, and again the evil pair were at her bedside.

This time it was a daughter, with eyes that shone like the sun. Again the two played their trick. This time a kitten replaced the baby, who was thrown into the river.

Now the king's anger was terrible. He ordered his wife to be executed, but his advisers pleaded with him – it was a misfortune, not a crime, they said. Instead she was locked in a tower, to weep alone.

Unknown to her, both children were safe. The girl, too, had been found by the gardener.

"She comes from the water – let us call her Yamuna," said his good wife.

And it was so. Chandra and Yamuna grew up together believing they were the gardener's children. They were kept from the world, and if they went beyond the walls of the garden Chandra was told to keep his forehead covered and Yamuna to keep her eyes lowered.

They lived to be handsome, lively and strong. Yamuna shared in all her brother's games, becoming as skilled at riding as he.

So the years passed and the old couple died, leaving brother and sister to tend the garden, content in the place where, for all they knew, they had been born.

But nothing remains for ever. One day a wandering woman, tired and thirsty, passed by and Yamuna gave her something to eat and drink and let her rest in the garden.

"You are a maiden from Heaven," said the old woman, "and I shall tell you a secret and give you gifts."

Yamuna smiled. "I need no gifts."

"Wait till you hear. I'll tell you where you can find golden water for your fountain, a singing tree for your garden and a talking bird to sit in its branches."

Quickly Yamuna called her brother to hear the story. The wanderer addressed herself to him: "If you ride to the East for twenty days and nights, you will find a wise man, who will tell you where to find these treasures."

With that she rose, blessed them and went away. And next day, Chandra saddled his horse and made ready for the journey. Now Yamuna began to have doubts.

"Chandra, take care. What good would marvels be if I lost you?" she said.

Chandra laughed. "Sister mine, have no fear. In forty days I shall return, bringing gifts."

And so, spurring his horse, he rode to the East and on the twentieth day he reached the foot of a bare mountain. There by the road stood an old man whose white hair hung to his waist.

"Greetings, O Chandra," he said.

"You know my name!" said the youth, astonished.

"I do, and I know why you have come."

"But how?"

"Many have passed this way before, just as you, seeking treasures. I know the look in your eyes. But none have returned, because none heeded my advice."

"I will listen," declared Chandra.

"See yonder mountain. Leave your horse and climb it. At the top are the treasures you seek. But you may get them only if you do not look behind you, and listen to no human voice."

Chandra laughed. The hill above them was bare save for many tall, upright rocks. No human being was in sight.

Dismounting, he began to climb. At first he went swiftly. But soon the way grew steeper, the sky above turned grey and a chill wind began to blow.

As he reached the first of the great rocks, to his amazement, he began to hear voices, as though the stones spoke, first in whispers, then in hoarse tones, then shouts and at last in shrieks.

"Turn back," said one. "Fool, you are doomed!" called another. "Help me, friend, help me!" pleaded a third. Their words tormented him and weighed down his spirit. But still he climbed till there came the awful cry, "Beware! Death stalks behind you!"

Chandra's hand leapt to his sword. He turned and, as he did, freezing cold flowed through his veins. His heart stopped and he was turned to stone, amid the other rocks.

On the fortieth day, Yamuna stood at the gate looking eastwards. To her joy she saw a horse trotting down the road. But as it came nearer she saw that the saddle was empty. Tears sprang to her eyes. Some dire fate had overtaken her brother.

But she would not allow fear and anguish to rule her. She led Chandra's horse to the stables. Then saddling her own mount she rode out, turning its head to the East, travelling by day and night, knowing neither hunger nor weariness.

After twenty days she came to the foot of the mountain and met the white-bearded man, who greeted her with pity.

"Yamuna, my child, must you suffer the same fate as your brother?"

"No, father," she answered, "I am here to save him and win the treasures he sought."

The venerable one sighed. "If you must venture up that dread mountain, then hear my counsel. Do not look back or listen to any human voice, not even if the one you have come here to save speaks to you."

At these words Yamuna's heart beat faster. Springing from her horse, she began the slow climb up the bare slope.

Grey was the sky, cold the wind and as she reached the rocks, so the air was full of voices, pleading, warning, threatening. But still she climbed, eyes on the summit, until one voice spoke softly: "Yamuna, turn to me. It is I, Chandra, behind you."

Almost she turned, but at the last second she tore a strip from her sleeve, divided it into two and thrust the rags into her ears. Now the voices, even Chandra's, ceased.

Again she climbed. But now the sky cleared, the sun shone and there on the mountain peak stood a tree whose leaves tinkled in the breeze. Beneath it played a fountain with water shining gold. In its branches sat a bird of brilliant colour. Now the bird opened its beak and spoke.

"Yamuna, the prize is yours. Take a twig from the tree and put it in your belt. Take that pitcher and fill it at the fountain."

"And you, talking bird?"

"I shall ride on your shoulder."

Yamuna did as she was directed. When the pitcher was full she went slowly down the mountain and as she walked she spilled a drop on each of the boulders.

The first, in an instant, changed into her brother Chandra. They embraced with delight. Soon every rock was transformed into a young man.

Proudly they took the homeward road. Singing Yamuna's praises, the rescued youths all returned to their families, while brother and sister rode back at last to their garden.

The twig, once planted, grew into a singing tree. Their fountain flowed with gold and in the branches the bird sat and talked. All as the old wandering woman had foretold.

But such wonders could not remain secret for long. Soon a messenger arrived, telling Chandra and Yamuna, "Prepare to receive your lord, the king!"

Barely had they spread a table beneath the tree when the king entered the garden. He sent away his courtiers and sat alone with Chandra and Yamuna, looking around him and marvelling.

"How can such wonders be?" he asked. "Is it not against nature?"

"How can you be so foolish, Majesty?" said the talking bird.

"Foolish?"

"A man who can easily believe his wife gave birth to animals, which is against nature, cannot believe in miracles?"

The king sprang up. "What is this?"

"Look at these two young people. They are your children. Chandra, take off your head scarf. Yamuna, raise your eyes."

The king gazed in stupefaction. "It is so, as my wife foretold. Oh, I have done wrong. How may I put it right?"

"Go swiftly," said the bird. "Go to the queen and fall on your knees before her, and beg her pardon. Above all, bring her back to meet her children for the first time."

So, the all-powerful king sped to do the bidding of a bird. The queen was set free and her enemies banished. Her joy when she saw her children knew no bounds, as if the terrible years had never been.

As for Yamuna and Chandra, though they lived as prince and princess in the royal palace, the garden, with its hard-won treasures, remained their favourite place.

Oonagh

Oonagh

....

Oonagh lived on Knockmany Hill with her
ever-loving husband Fin M'Coul.

No one knew why Fin had built their house
up there among the clouds, where the wind
blew day and night. He said he enjoyed the
view, though Oonagh suspected there was
some other reason he wasn't telling her
about.

Worse still, there was no water to be had on
the hill top. Fin was always promising to sink
a well. But it never got dug.

And where was he now? At the other end of
Ireland with a band of other giants building a
great rock causeway over the sea to Scotland!

To while away the time in his absence,
Oonagh chatted now and then with her sister
Granua, who lived on Cullamore across the
valley. It was three or four miles away, but

that was no problem if they just raised their voices a little.

One evening Granua said, "Would you believe it sister? Who d'you think's coming up the road, no more than fifty miles away."

"Tell me, sister, tell me."

"Why, your ever-loving man, Fin M'Coul."

"What can he want now? Surely they've not built all the way over to Scotland already?"

"You'll find out soon enough, sister," said Granua.

Sure enough, before the sun was down, in through the door came Fin, calling out, "God save all here."

"Welcome home, Fin my darling," said Oonagh, giving him a kiss that stirred up waves on the lake down at the foot of Knockmany.

"And how are you, beautiful one?" asked her husband.

"As merry a wife as ever there was," answered Oonagh. "And what brings you home so soon?"

Fin looked at her a little oddly but laughed. "Just love and affection for yourself, you know that."

But after two or three happy days had passed, Oonagh, who was nobody's fool, could see something was wrong with her husband. So she set to work to wheedle it out of him. And at last he confessed.

"It's this Cucullin. For months he's been rampaging round Ireland looking to destroy me. They say he's flattened a thunderbolt to a pancake and carries it in his pocket to show what he's going to do to my head – if I let him come near enough."

"So that is why we live up here, Fin?"

"That's it, my love. So I can see him coming."

"But, he's far away, surely to goodness?"

Fin shook his head and put his thumb in his mouth and began to chew it. For his thumb could tell him what or who was to come his way.

"Don't draw blood now, my dear," said his wife.

Fin took out his thumb. "Cucullin's coming. I can see him below Dungannon. He'll be here by two o'clock tomorrow." He groaned. "What shall I do? If I run away, I'm disgraced as a coward. If I stay, I'm dead mutton."

Oonagh looked at him fondly. "Don't be cast down, my love. I'll think of something a bit smarter than your rule of thumb."

She went to the door and called out over the valley, "What can you see, sister?"

Back came the answer, "The biggest giant that ever was, coming up from Dungannon. What can he want, now?"

"He's on his way to leather our Fin!"

"Is he now. Well, Oonagh, I'll invite him in for a meal and detain him a little to give you time to think of something. Knowing you, I'm sure you'll get the better of him."

So saying, Granua put fingers to her lips and gave three whistles, which was a polite way of inviting the unwelcome guest to tarry awhile and take pot luck with her.

Now Oonagh busied herself. She spun threads of nine different colours, dividing them into three plaits. One plait she tied round her arm, one round her heart and one round her ankle. With these charms she was ready for anything and anybody.

Next she set dough and put down a great pot of milk to make curds and whey, while Fin watched her and grumbled, "Are you going to *feed* the brute before he murders me?"

"Oh, Fin, I'm ashamed of you," said his wife. "Leave Cucullin to me. I'll give him a meal like he's never had in his life. Trust Oonagh."

Out she went to her neighbours in the mountains round about – it took her no more than a minute or two – and borrowed twenty-one griddle irons. As she made up the loaves she put an iron inside each, save one. Then she set them all to bake.

"Now, Fin, my lad," said she, "get the baby's clothes on and lie down in the cradle. Pretend to be your own child. Don't say a word. Just listen while I tell you what to do. Trust Oonagh."

Fin was humiliated. But that's a shade better than being flattened. So he did as he was told.

All too soon in walked the giant Cucullin saying, "God save all here. Is this the home of Fin M'Coul?"

"It is," replied Oonagh. "Tell me – from the stern look on your face – is there something wrong concerning my husband?"

"Not at all." Cucullin leered at Oonagh. "It's just that he has the reputation of being strongest in all Ireland and I'd like to put that to the test. But I can't seem to catch up with the man."

"And no wonder," said Oonagh very quickly, "for you're looking in entirely the wrong direction. He heard you were down at the Giant's Causeway and off he went there in a hurry."

"Well," said Cucullin, rising, "when I get my hands on him..."

But Oonagh only laughed. "Sit down, now. You never saw Fin, I can tell. And if you'll take my advice, you'll pray that you never do. For he's mad to lay hands on you."

She looked round. "Drat that wind. It's blowing right through the door again and my husband's not here to turn the house round as he always does for me when the wind shifts. Can you be civil enough to do it instead?"

Cucullin's mouth dropped open for a moment. But, not to be outfaced, he got up, cracked his middle finger (where his power lay) three times, then grabbed the house by the corners and swung it round on its foundations.

That shook Oonagh a little, and what it did to Fin, crouched in the cradle, can just be imagined.

"That's decent of you," she said calmly. "Now, before I offer you something to eat, can you do me a second favour? Fin's been so busy lately chasing after you, he's had no time to sink me a well for water. Just four hundred feet would do, no more."

Her guest's jaw dropped at this, but pride would not let him refuse. Out he went, cracked his strength finger nine times and tore a great cleft a quarter of a mile long and four hundred foot deep in the ground, which is still there for anyone to see.

"Now," said Oonagh, satisfied, "pray sit down and eat." She set bacon and cabbage and a great pile of new-baked loaves on the table.

Hungry as a wolf, Cucullin snatched up a loaf and stuffed it into his mouth. But the next moment he was howling with pain and spitting out his best teeth.

"Blood and fury," he bellowed, "what have you put in these loaves?"

Oonagh shrugged. "Why, they're just what my husband – and the baby – always eat. See."

And with that she offered a loaf (the one without a griddle iron in it, of course) to Fin in the cradle. He, falling in with the trick, made it vanish in a trice.

The guest was thunderstruck. "Let's have a look at that infant," he growled.

Oonagh gave Fin the nod and he stepped out of his cradle. He looked a complete fool in the swaddling clothes, but Cucullin did not find him comical at all.

"What size must the father be," he asked, "if this be the child?"

"Pray you'll never find out," said Fin, beginning to enjoy the joke. "In my father's absence, will you go a trial of strength with me? Can you squeeze water out of this little white stone?"

Well Cucullin squeezed that white stone till he almost burst a blood vessel, but not a drop of moisture came out of it.

Fin now took up a handful of Oonagh's white curds. This he squeezed until the clear whey liquid ran down for all the world like water. Then, with a look of silent contempt for Cucullin, he climbed back into his cradle.

That man's knees now began to knock

together. "I'll be off," he said, "and kindly tell your husband I shall make myself scarce and hope not to meet him."

But before he left he could not resist one last question. "The baby's teeth must be made of iron to eat that bread of yours. Can I have a look at them?"

"You can do more. You can put your middle finger right in and feel them," invited Oonagh.

This he did. And Fin needed no invitation. He closed his teeth and snapped off the visitor's strength finger, clean as a whistle. In a trice, Cucullin's power was gone, and so was he, running away down the mountain.

So it came about that Cucullin, the terror, ceased to bother Fin. And all thanks to Oonagh.

Janet

Janet

Late summer sun shone on the lawn below the castle. Courtiers leaned on the walls idly talking. Girls ran laughing to and fro, tossing a ball to one another.

But Janet, the king's daughter, stood apart, looking down the valley to a strange little wood where the birch trees gleamed silver midst the green.

"What are you thinking of, lady?" asked a young courtier. Janet did not turn her head, but answered, "I'm looking down to Carterhaugh. Of a sudden, I have such a longing to be there."

"Put such thoughts from you, Highness," said a grey-bearded knight. "You know your father warned all maidens not to go near that place with its darkness, its deep well."

Janet looked at him coolly. "That's just an

old story, is it not?"

The old man answered sternly, "It's no place for a damsel ripe to wed. No such maid is safe from Tam Lin, the elfin knight. If you should chance to meet him, you'd bring dire misfortune upon us all."

Janet smiled but did not answer. She knew what was in the greybeard's mind. He had ambitions to marry her and that she would never agree to – no, not till oranges grew on an apple tree.

Besides, who was this old knight to tell her what she should do?

Stooping, she gathered her green skirts above her knee and tied them there. Then, binding her golden hair with a scarf round her forehead, she strode away into the dell.

Out of the sun, the woodland gloom was cold. Janet shivered, then laughed at herself, moving on across the carpet of soft turf. A path lay before her. She took it, turning now left, now right.

As she came out into a small glade, faintly

dappled with sunlight, she gasped. In the middle of the clearing stood a well, ringed round with moss-covered stone, and hung over with briars and a cloud of red, red roses.

She reached out to pick one. But as she did, there came the jingle of harness. Turning, she saw a riderless horse, white as milk, with legs so slender it seemed like a steed from a dream. Its hooves glinted silver and gold in the half light.

Even as she looked, the dream horse snorted and vanished into the twilight of the trees. Janet sighed. Her heart was full of strange excitement.

Again she put out a hand and this time she plucked a rose. And as she did, there came a voice: "Who calls me?"

Janet turned. Close by her, so close she could touch him, was a man. She had never seen a youth so handsome nor so finely dressed, with a face so noble. But his grey eyes were sad.

Now he smiled. "It is you, Burd Janet. I

have seen you looking out from the castle walls."

"You know my name?"

"I do."

"Then I know yours. You are Tam Lin."

"And are you not afraid?"

"Not I. I wished to meet you. Tam Lin, where is your home?"

"I have no home. I may not leave this place."

Janet reached out to him wonderingly. The arms she touched were flesh. This was no spirit. They embraced, and those arms were strong.

"Who *are* you, Tam Lin?"

He looked around him, then spoke in low tones. "My grandfather was the Lord Roxburgh. We went hunting one winter day. I wandered from the others in this wood. My horse threw me and when I woke again, the Elf Queen had me in her arms. Now I am her knight and slave."

"If you cannot leave this place, then I will

stay with you," said Janet, for she knew she loved Tam Lin.

His lips touched hers. He shook his head. "You will go back to your own folk, Janet, I know."

"But, not yet, not yet," she answered, and they lay down on the mossy ground beneath the roses.

There was a whispering round the castle: the princess was going to have a baby.

The greybeard knight's face was grim. "It is as I said, lady. You have brought shame on us all. Only marriage can make it well again. You must marry me at once."

"Hold your tongue," said Janet sharply. "Whatever becomes of me, I'll not name you the father of any child of mine."

"Janet, Janet," the king himself spoke mildly. "You are with child and that's the truth, and the child must be seen to have a father. You *must* marry."

"A father it has indeed," she answered,

"but I shan't pretend he's any lord from your court. I would not exchange my elfin knight for any on earth."

And with that Janet strode from the court. Running like the wind, her skirts looped up, her yellow hair flying, she came at last to the well in Carterhaugh.

But no horse was there. The glade was empty, silent as the grave. Boldly Janet put out her hand and plucked a red, red rose. But no one came.

Her fingers were round the stem of a second rose when a hand held her back. Tam Lin was there.

"Janet! Hold! Pluck a second rose and you kill our child."

"Our child shall live, Tam Lin, and we shall wed, on earth or in Elf-land, above ground or below."

He put a finger to her lips.

"It may not be, Janet. It may not be."

"Why may it not, Tam Lin?"

His grey eyes grew darker. "Every seven

years Elf-land and its queen must make a sacrifice to Hell, of the fairest one among the faery court."

"And that is you, Tam Lin?" said Janet, in dread.

"I fear so."

"That shall not be." She took his hand. "Is there no way to escape this doom?"

"There is a chance, the faintest chance."

"Tell me, Tam Lin."

He looked at her long and hard. "You are my true love, Janet. Can you do this thing for me? It will take more courage than has ever been asked of you in your life."

"I can, I will."

"On Hallowe'en the elfin court will ride. You must wait for us at the crossroads, at midnight. Step forward boldly as I ride past. Pull me down from my horse, thrust me into pure stream water and cover me with your cloak."

"I will do all that. But how shall I know you from among them all?"

"First will ride a black horse, then a brown. And after that my own milk-white steed. My left hand will be ungloved, my helmet raised to show my face. Take hold of me, Janet. Do not forsake me."

"I shall not, never fear."

"But the Elf Queen will not let me go so easily. She'll work her spells. Whatever happens, clasp me in your arms. Take hold and fear not. I am the father of your child."

Janet kissed her love once more.

"Tam Lin, I will be there."

The owl hoot died away. An eerie silence fell where four lanes met in darkness. Hidden in the bushes, Janet shivered – and heard a distant clop of horses' hooves. The sound came closer, ever closer, and before long the elfin procession was in sight and bearing down on her.

First stepped the coal black horse and on its back, proud and tall, her green eyes gleaming, sat the Elf Queen. So awesome was that look, Janet trembled again. But she held her ground while the second rider passed.

Then, as the white steed trotted up, she sprang from the bushes and dragged her lover from the saddle.

All was confusion, shouts, horses neighing and plunging. But her arms were round Tam Lin.

And then her love for him was all but overwhelmed with terror. For as she held him close, his skin began to change, his arms sprouted harsh scales, his fingers claws. Horror and disgust shook her. But still she would not let go.

For in her head she heard Tam's voice: "Hold fast and do not fear me."

As she tightened her grip, the giant lizard was gone and in her arms, hissing and writhing, spitting in her face, was a snake. Almost she threw it from her, but yet held on.

Skin changed to rough, dark fur, serpent length to bear's enormous bulk. Fangs and claws tore at her till she screamed with pain.

But above that she heard Tam Lin's voice in her heart: "I am the father of your child."

The bear vanished. Now blistering heat seared her hands. Between them a long iron bar shone white as from a furnace. Her hair, her clothes, were on fire.

"Do not forsake me. Fear me not."

Tighter still she grasped the white-hot bar and in her fingers it shrank to the size of a burning coal. She cried out in triumph. Running to the stream, she flung it from her. It struck the water in a cloud of vapour.

And there, white skin shining in the light of the newly risen moon, was Tam Lin, her love, naked as the day he was born. Unclasping her cloak, Janet threw it round him. Tam was safe in her arms.

Harness jingled above her. The Elf Queen looked down from the saddle. Eyes like ice were fixed not on Janet, but on Tam Lin.

"Had I known, Tam Lin, had I known this would happen, I'd have put out your eyes. Never would you have seen Burd Janet."

She wheeled her mount and called out her commands. In a moment the elf host had vanished. Janet and her Tam Lin were alone.

Tam Lin bent and kissed Janet's hand. "I owe you my life, lady," said he.

She smiled at him. "Then share it with me. Come, let us go to my father's house."

Before dawn they were safe within the castle walls.

Zumurrud

Zumurrud

....

In the land of Khorosan, there lived a girl who was fair, witty and wise. Yet she was a slave. Her master, however, was kind and while she worked in his house she was able to save a little money for, who knew, one day she might be free.

The time came, though, when the master fell on bad times and was obliged to put his household on the market. Zumurrud's heart sank at this, for she knew other masters were as harsh as he was good-hearted.

He said to her, "My child, I shall order it so that you shall choose your own master. I can do no more."

So, one morning, Zumurrud stood in the market. Around the square stood merchants, officials and idlers all eyeing the slaves, not least Zumurrud. They liked what they saw.

She looked back and did not care for them at all.

."Who will give five hundred dinars for this pearl?" called the Master of the Market. The crowd answered in chorus, "I will."

Soon the bidding raised the price to eight hundred dinars and only two could pay that price. Her master asked Zumurrud, "Which shall it be, fair one – this worthy merchant or the Venerable Rashid al Din?"

Zumurrud shook her head. "Neither. One is too fat, the other has one foot in the grave and has not cleaned his beard today."

The crowd laughed. Even the fat merchant smiled. But Rashid al Din's eyes glittered with fury.

Now Zumurrud pointed to a tall slender young man on the edge of the square.

The master said, "Ali Shah, son of a silk dealer now – alas – gone from us. A good choice."

But the youth called out, "I thank you, I shall not buy," and turned away.

Zumurrud said, "Let me talk to him," and she ran to Ali Shah.

"Do I displease you sir?" she whispered.

He answered softly, "No, no. You are fair and witty. But I do not even have eight dinars to my name. I have no shop, no house, only debts. Seek your buyer elsewhere and may Heaven be kind to you."

Zumurrud answered, "O Ali Shah, do as I say. Put your arm round my waist as a sign that you will buy. On my girdle is a purse with one thousand dinars. Take them, pay my price. Then go, rent a room, buy food. Tonight we shall be together."

He smiled, "Your words are like honey. But what of tomorrow?"

Zumurrud answered, "Tomorrow – is another day."

Next day Zumurrud greeted Ali Shah, "Morning of goodness, O Ali Shah."

He answered, "Morning of Light, O Zumurrud." But his voice was sad.

"Are you unhappy? Did you not sleep well?"

Ali Shah groaned. "I did not sleep at all. I am a fool. I wasted all the wealth my father left me, drinking with false friends. I have not enough to keep body and soul together and now there are two mouths to feed." Speaking solemnly, he continued, "Zumurrud, take your freedom, go and seek your fortune in better hands."

Zumurrud only laughed. "Do not add more foolishness to your folly. Listen to me. Take the fifty dinars that remain. Go to the market and buy red Damascus silk, thread of gold, silver, green and blue, needles and a thimble. Go."

Ali Shah did as he was bid and watched, eyes wide, as Zumurrud transformed this material into a wall hanging with a vivid hunting scene. Before nightfall, Ali Shah, using the skills learned from his father, had sold this on the market for two hundred dinars.

Next day was the same, and the next. Zumurrud embroidered, Ali Shah sold. They prospered, bought a shop, a house and lived as master and mistress. Old friends of his father complimented Ali Shah but he answered wherever he went, "The credit is not mine but clever Zumurrud's."

His happiness knew no bounds. But one day it came to an end. Returning to his home after a successful day's trading, he found it empty. Zumurrud the fair was gone.

He searched house, garden, and street, and for three days and nights wandered round the city like a mad man, asking people, calling her name.

On the fourth day when he was sick with despair a man came to him. "Ali Shah," the man whispered, "your loved one has been kidnapped. She is in the harem of Rashid al Din."

Ali Shah leapt up. "I'll go there and have his life!"

"No, no, no!" The man restrained him. "He has many slaves. Besides he is a crony of the

Chief of Police. But I can arrange her escape..."

"Name your price."

"Five hundred dinars now, five hundred when she is back in your arms."

"Done, done."

"Very well. Tomorrow the moon rises late. Be in the Street of the Four Camels behind Rashid al Din's house. I will bribe the eunuch in charge of the harem. At midnight, Zumurrud, who is a lively girl, will climb over the wall and be with you before the moon shows herself."

Ali Shah did as he was instructed. In a fever of longing, he hid outside Rashid al Din's harem wall as darkness fell. But alas, worn out by long searching and distress, he fell asleep.

Thus it happened that at midnight, as Zumurrud climbed over the wall, she fell into the arms, not of her beloved, but of someone else. El Javan, robber chief, brutal and ugly, returning from evil-doing, saw the lovely maid as she climbed down the wall.

Shouting, "This is my lucky night," he seized her and carried her away. When Ali Shah woke it was daylight and he was alone.

Cursing his folly, he began his search once more. But now he must look further afield. He sold house and shop and began to wander through the land asking after her.

Next day Zumurrud found herself in the robber camp. The men were away raiding and she was guarded by a foul old woman. But, telling herself not to despair, Zumurrud set out to make friends with the crone.

She offered to comb her clotted hair. Delighted, her guardian sat down while Zumurrud, with gritted teeth, groomed her till the beldame fell fast asleep.

In a trice, Zumurrud had found men's clothes, taken one of the robber's horses and was galloping away.

Riding and resting, she travelled three days, seeking always to come beyond the reach of the bandits. On the fourth day she approached a splendid, walled city.

As she drew near she saw a great, gaily dressed crowd coming to meet her, crying out, "Long live the king!"

"What does this mean, good sirs?" asked Zumurrud, climbing wearily from her horse.

They answered with smiles, "O, fortunate youth. It is our custom when our ruler dies to invite the first stranger who arrives at our gates to take his place. What is your name, young sir?"

"Hassan," replied Zumurrud quickly.

The crowd roared, "Long live King Hassan!"

A year passed. King Hassan's wisdom pleased all his subjects, though the maidens puzzled why so handsome a prince should sleep on his own, indeed would allow no servants in his bed chamber.

And King Hassan had other strange ways. Every month all citizens were invited, together with travellers, to a banquet served on carpets spread before the city gates. Seated on the throne, the king looked down on the feasting multitude.

One day in mid-feast he called out, "That old man with his paws in the rice cream pot! Bring him to me."

This was done and the king asked him, "Who are you?"

He replied, "My name, Majesty, is Haroun, a humble pilgrim."

"Liar!" roared the king. "You are Rashid al Din, slavemaster and kidnapper of Zumurrud, whom even now you seek. Throw him into the dungeons!"

At the next banquet the same happened. A bearded traveller was seized at the king's command, even as his hand was in the rice pudding.

"Who are you?"

He replied, "I am Yusuf, a travelling shoemaker."

"Liar!" thundered the king. "You are the wicked robber, El Javan. Away with him!"

All these things were marvels to the king's

subjects. And when at the next banquet, a slender young man, travel-stained and hungry, began to eat the rice cream, his fellow guests begged him to leave it alone.

Too late. He was marched to the king and asked his name. He answered, "Majesty, I am Ali Shah, desperately seeking my Zumurrud, lost through my own folly."

The king nodded. "That is true. Take this young man, see he is bathed, given new clothes and led to my chamber. Eyebrows were raised at this as the young man, pale and bewildered, was led away.

Changed and bathed, Ali Shah sat outside the royal bedroom. His heart was heavy. What could this mean?

Soon he was led inside and stood before the king's bed. From behind the curtains came a command: "Ali Shah, handsome one, take off your clothes and come here to me."

He trembled. "O Prince, I dare not."

The voice became firmer. "Ah, but you must."

"Majesty," pleaded Ali Shah, "I shall die if I do."

Back came the answer: "And I shall die if you do not!"

The curtains were thrown back. Ali Shah stared, open-mouthed. "Zumurrud!" he cried.

Zumurrud stepped from the bed and looked down. "O Ali Shah, I have waited for you so long. But now we are together at last."

Marian

Marian

At dawn, when Sherwood was white as snow with hawthorn blossom, the townsfolk came, as they had done since old time, to fell their may tree in the forest.

Horns blew, pipes shrieked, drums pounded and there was a great clamour of shouting and singing.

First marched men in green and yellow smocks, the axeman leading them. Behind, creaking and rumbling, rolled the wagon drawn by oxen, their horns festooned with ribbons.

And after them marched a great unruly crowd, old and young, led by a girl, tall and straight, her yellow hair bound with a circlet of flowers.

The procession left the sunlit meadow and

plunged into the forest shade. In the gloom the sounds of celebration died away, only the creaking of the wagon wheels broke the silence.

Before them the trees opened into a great glade, which now slowly filled with quietened folk. Some looked this way and that at the trees and bushes that ringed them round so darkly.

Pressing forward, the tall girl took from her waist a long sash. Choosing a straight and slender tree, she looped the girdle round its trunk, calling out, "We choose our may tree as by right!" Turning to the axeman, she commanded, "Strike!"

But the man did not. He looked round, listening, hand to ear.

"Are we safe here, Marian? I heard in the town that the sheriff's men would be out. They may be lying in wait for us."

"What do we care for the sheriff's men?" retorted Marian.

But the man's head wagged. "You know,

Marian, that the new law says we may not take green in the royal woods without the sheriff gives us leave."

Marian looked at him with disdain. "A fig for your new law! Strike, man!"

But still the axeman would not. His ears were tuned to the forest silence. And suddenly there was a rustle in the bushes, a faint sound like a man clearing his throat.

"I was right," the axeman declared. "The sheriff's men are lying in ambush. We shall be trapped and beaten – if we are not put in irons in the castle."

Marian frowned. "Stand firm. We are many. They are few."

More rustling in the undergrowth and the axeman said, "I'm away."

Throwing down the blade, he pushed his way through the crowd. As he did, there came suppressed chuckles from the green thickets – and the axeman's friends turned tail and ran, too.

"Cowards!" raged Marian, snatching up the axe herself.

"Harsh words, my child," an unctuous, fruity voice spoke from the bushes. Out into the clearing stepped the strangest figure. Not a sheriff's man at arms, nor a woodman in his jerkin, but a jolly fat monk, brown habit bulging, belly tied in with a rope.

At the sight of him the townsfolk calmed and stood their ground. One old man spoke cheerfully: "It's Friar Tuck."

"No more, no less," responded the hedge priest. "Greetings, good people all. Robin Hood bids you welcome to the forest to take your may tree as by right."

"What of the sheriff's men?" asked the old one.

As if in answer, the bushes bent, as a giant in green – staff in hand – stepped out. "Far away, if they've any sense. But if they come back, Little John'll warm their backsides for them!"

"Will Scarlett, too," said a third voice, and

a red-clad man with bright sword in hand appeared.

Now the glade was ringed with men in green and Marian laughed out loud. "We thank you all for your protection. But will your master honour us with his presence?"

"He is behind you."

Turning, Marian saw a handsome outlaw, little older than she, a lean dark face fringed with beard, eyes keen and challenging.

She curtsied, then picked up the axe and held it out.

"Be pleased to fell our tree, good sir."

The town square swarmed with people. Beneath the church's sandstone walls, long tables were heaped with food. Little John licked his lips. "Meat, spiced pastries, new-baked bread and ale – so much ale," he said.

Friar Tuck nudged him. "Be still, you gannet. Eating comes later."

Cheers rose in the air as the may tree, rolled

from the wagon, was stepped up in mid-square, secured with ropes and hung with garlands.

Someone shouted, "A chain, a chain!"

Girls broke from the crowd and took the outlaws with them. Marian turned to Robin. They joined hands. Pipe and drum shrilled and thundered and the crowd transformed itself into a dancing snake, reeling round and round, in and out of the churchyard.

"A ring, a ring!" came the call and soon two circles formed, men in one, women in the other. Slowly the music and the laughter stilled and a girl began to sing:

Maiden in the woods lay,
    seven nights, seven nights,
Maiden in the woods lay,
    seven nights and a day.
Well was her bed, what was her bed?
Red rose and a violet.

The circles turned like wheels, faster and faster.

Well was her love, who was her love?
May King and a May King.

The circles came to rest, Marian and Robin opposite one another.

"May Queen! May King!" shouted the crowd.

Marian took Robin and led him to an oak-wood seat by the church wall. As they sat down, girls threw flowers over them. Friar Tuck waddled forward. In his hands were circlets of cowslip and marsh marigold. As he raised them, the crowd was silent again.

"In the name of Heaven's king and queen," he intoned, "I crown you, Robin, and you, Marian, May King and Queen. Peace and Plenty attend you."

Then, addressing the crowd, the friar called, "Come one, come all, here shall none suffer loss. Here shall be justice and more than fair dealing. Here shall be no penny loaves, only tenpenny loaves. Here shall be no small beer, only strong ale."

The feasting began. In the hot afternoon sun, the air was heavy with the scent of crushed blossom. Marian and Robin laughed together, toasted one another and kissed.

But in a while Marian's voice grew quiet and earnest.

"Robin, you and your band live free in the forest. So would I."

He shook his head. "We have no maids with us. Those who have sweethearts must go home to them, in secret, when the time is ripe."

"Why so?"

"Women should not live like thieves, bow and sword in hand."

"I am not afraid," said she.

He smiled. "That I know. But we are outlaws. Sheriff's men may take us, if they can, hang us and leave our bodies swaying in the wind. That's no fate for a maid."

"Girls can be strong if they choose."

Robin shook his head. "All's well when the sun shines, but when the winter winds blow..."

Marian spoke angrily. "You think I am just

fit for dancing in the street. I tell you, what any man can stand, I'll endure."

Robin turned away from her as Will Scarlett laid a hand on his shoulder, face stern.

"Robin, the sheriff's men are marching from the castle, fifty-strong."

Robin sprang to his feet. "Listen to me lads," he shouted. "We must away to the greenwood."

"Why so?" demanded Little John.

"The sheriff's men are coming."

"Let 'em come. We'll whip them home again."

Robin shook his head angrily.

"We may fight, John. But look around you – children, old folk. If we are here, the sheriff's men will kill without mercy all in their path." He raised his voice. "No, lads. Drink up. Say farewell and let's be gone."

Grumbling, the outlaws rose from the table and followed their leader. Marian ran after him and made one last plea.

"Take me with you, Robin!"

Again he shook his head. "It may not be. It is our law." He kissed her. "Farewell, we'll meet again."

She eyed him boldly. "Aye we will." And to herself she added, "Sooner than you think, Robin Hood."

As she went about her daily tasks, Marian thought of the outlaw band and their free life in the greenwood. She longed for a taste of that life, even just for a season, and that she was determined to have, whether the stern, handsome leader willed it or not. But how?

One night, as she lay awake, she made up her mind what to do, and the next day, before the sun was up, she left her bed. Dressed in clothes borrowed from her brother, she belted on her father's sword.

Pulling down her hood to mask her face, she stole from home and soon Sherwood forest's green depths took her in. An hour's journey by twisting tracks would bring her to the camp. But would Robin's men turn her away when she reached it?

There was one way they could not refuse her. And that she meant to try.

A faint familiar sound caught her ear. A man was walking by himself, whistling softly. Creeping from the path, she waited in hiding.

A green-clad figure strolled towards her. His head was bent, but Marian did not doubt who it might be. Bending her own head, she stepped into the other's way and walked on steadily.

He spoke mildly. "This path's wide enough. Give way a little, sir, and I'll make room for you."

Marian did not answer, only pressing on. Now the outlaw spoke more sternly. "Is this a challenge, boy? If so, it's on your own head."

Now was the moment of truth and Marian braced herself for it. There was a rasp of steel from Robin Hood and she too drew sword. Raising her head, she lunged at her opponent. He grinned and parried the thrust. The grin enraged her. She swung furiously. Blood sprang from his forehead, appalling her.

As her blade faltered, his leapt forward. She felt a savage pain. Her head spun and she fell.

Voices aroused her. Faces in a circle looked down. Friar Tuck's round features were alarmed.

"Robin! It's Marian! Have you killed her? Quick, lift her up, lads, and carry her to the Trysting Tree. There I've my medicines and ointments. Look lively."

Teeth clenched against the pain, but smiling to herself, Marian was brought into the camp and laid on the soft green turf. Anxious men gathered round.

"Pray Heaven, you've not killed the maid, Robin," said Little John.

Marian opened her eyes.

"Praise be," said Tuck. "She will live. But

she must stay in our camp for some little time."

Now Marian knew her challenge, though risky, had succeeded. Her eyes met Robin's, smiling. He understood and first he frowned, then smiled, then laughed aloud.

"Welcome to our band, brave Marian," he said.

So Marian stayed with Robin for a while. No need for marriage, said Tuck, for those who had been crowned May King and Queen in the shadow of the church.

But when the smoke from the midsummer fires had died away, Marian went back to her own folk.

"We'll meet again in spring," she promised Robin.